Dexter's Journey

First published in Great Britain 2000 by Mammoth
an imprint of Egmont Children's Books Limited
239 Kensington High Street, London W8 6SA.
Published in hardback by Heinemann Library,
a division of Reed Educational and Professional Publishing Limited
by arrangement with Egmont Children's Books Limited.
Text copyright © Chris d'Lacey 2000
Illustrations © David Roberts 2000
The Author and Illustrator have asserted their moral rights.
Paperback ISBN 0 7497 4098 1
Hardback ISBN 0 431 06983 2
10 9 8 7 6 5 4 3 2 1
A CIP catalogue record for this title is available from the British Library.
Printed in Dubai.

Dexter's Journey

Chris d'Lacey

Illustrated by David Roberts

Blue Bananas

For Alice Georgina
because she's quackers!
C.d'L.

For Lauren and Simon
D.R.

Once upon a bathtime, there was a yellow plastic duck called Dexter . . .

. . . who was about to go on a long, long journey.

It started on a ship that was sailing to America. Dexter and a lot of other little ducks were packed tightly into a large wooden crate. There was hardly room for a duck to quack.

Then . . . CRASH! It slid overboard! And all the little ducks went bobbing out to sea!

The sea went on for ever

and ever . . .

. . . for ever and

ever and ever

and ever. . .

Bob for it!

One morning, some hungry seagulls
appeared. They were circling in the grey
sky, searching for food.

They saw the ducks and came
swooping down.

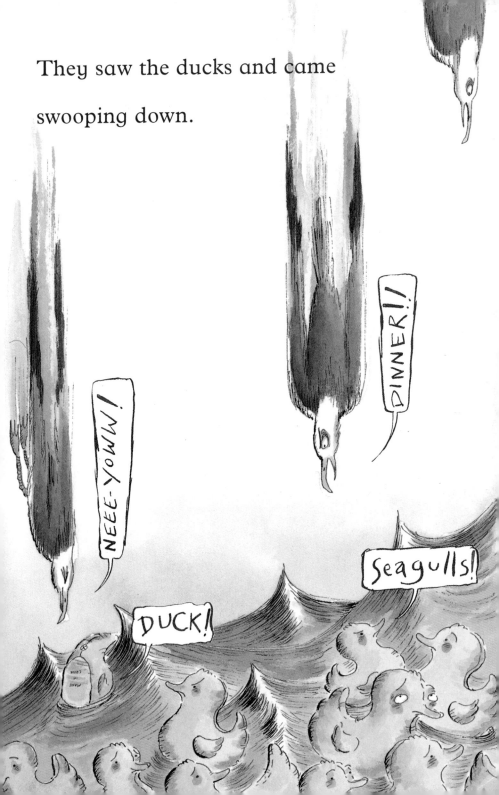

The ducks bobbed bravely but couldn't get away. Dozens were snatched from the open waves and carried away to the seagulls' nests!

Fortunately, they were a bit

too chewy to eat.

So the seagulls went off looking for fish. The ducks were left all alone on the cliffs.

It was cold and windy. The sea was
crashing on the rocks below. The ducks
were frightened, and a little bit dizzy.

Luckily, some rock climbers were out

that day.

They put the ducks safely into their

rucksacks.

Later, they gave them as presents to their children.

But Dexter was still in the water, bobbing.

That afternoon a fishing boat came
chugging by. It was trailing a great big
net behind it. Hundreds of fish were
wriggling in the net. Soon something
else got in there too . . . .

When the fishermen got home they didn't

know what to do with their catch.

But Old Joe Salty had a good idea.

He took the ducks to a travelling fair,

so the children could play "hook a duck"

and win them. This made the ducks

very happy.

But Dexter was still on the ocean, bobbing.

Soon, night fell. The moon cast a misty trail across the ocean. It was freezing cold, and getting foggy too. The ducks huddled together and fell fast asleep.

But when morning came there was ice
all around them! The sea had frozen and
the ducks were stuck! Some of them were
even hidden in a snowdrift!

Fortunately, a Norwegian explorer was passing by.

He chipped out all the ducks he could find and piled them up in a heap on his sledge. Dexter quacked and quacked but the explorer didn't hear him.

The explorer took the ducks home to Norway. He showed schoolchildren pictures of where he'd found them . . .

. . . then gave them one each.

But Dexter was still stuck in the snow.

Soon the Arctic sun came out. The
snowdrift melted and the ice began
to crack. The ducks played a game
of tag between the ice floes.

Then a huge polar bear came lolloping by.

He wanted to play his own game of tag!

There was nowhere the ducks could

escape to – except . . .

. . . under the ice! The ducks held their breaths and tumbled along. They tumbled towards a tiny, bright hole . . .

Sploop! It was Uluk the hunter's fishing hole! Uluk was so surprised at his catch, he nearly fell into the hole!

One by one, Uluk picked the ducks out.
Then he put them into his parka and
took them to a trading post. He swapped
them for a pair of boots!

The trader put the ducks on the shelves of her store. She sold them to people who came visiting on their holidays.

But Dexter wasn't up for sale. He wasn't
in the trading post . . .

He wasn't in Uluk's fishing hole . .

Dexter was ALL ALONE on the ocean!

He drifted along for days and days.

He saw a few bits of wood

. . . some twinkling stars

. . . a message in a bottle

. . . and two confused shrimps.

I'm Jim.

I'm Jim you're Tim

Then one morning something came up.

It was a submarine's periscope.

Dexter swam up close to the periscope.

And this is what the crew of the

submarine saw . . .

With a whoosh the submarine rose to the surface. Captain Toffee walked along the hull. 'That's not a giant duck!' he laughed. 'It's one of those plastic ones that were lost in the storm.'

And he picked Dexter up and popped him

in his cap . . .

. . . then took him home to his grandson, George.

That was the end of Dexter's journey.

Now he sits in George's bathroom,

thinking about his adventures and

waiting for George to have his bath.